The Accounts of the Scorned

The Accounts of the Scorned

Jeh Wells

iUniverse, Inc.
Bloomington

The Accounts of the Scorned

iUniverse books may be ordered through booksellers or by contacting:

iUniverse
1663 Liberty Drive
Bloomington, IN 47403
www.iuniverse.com
1-800-Authors (1-800-288-4677)

ISBN: 978-1-4620-1726-3 (pbk)
ISBN: 978-1-4620-1727-0 (ebk)

Printed in the United States of America

iUniverse rev. date:05/26/11

My dedications

First and for most thanks to God the most high, for if not for his blessing this book wouldn't be possible. To my mother and father who gave me life. For Shamyra, Xizmenna and Azureé my crazy sisters who make me laugh I love you all with my whole heart. To my little brother Jahkeem who is wise beyond his years, go get "that watch that don't tock". To "Kerry" keep your head up, don't let anything stop you from achieving your goals. To "Keith's wife" who's passing will open the eyes of many women. To Dré and Brea you were the first two people to read Keith's wife the day after it was written thank you, I love you both. To "Shelly" Smith you're a tattoo and you're proof love can transcend time. For D.M Parkinson because you are a genuinely great man and any woman who is fortunate enough to have you is blessed; P.S Like the song says "I guess I'll see you next life time." Last but not least for those who ever wanted to see me fall; I made it and I love you all too.

Dear Dr. Dillard,

I loved him and still I love him. Even in death he is my poison. Leaving upon me marks that no one else could fathom. We were married for ten years, he never wanted children for reasons he wouldn't explain and despite that fact I still loved him. He was all over town doing God knows what, with God knows who. But he always came home on time and knowing this I still loved him. The calls from his many women haunted my house like ghosts. I drank it all in and still said nothing. Until one day my phone started to ring differently. Not only were women calling our home but men as well . . .

My resilience turned to shame as the voice on the end other echoed in my ears "your little husband bitch, I hope you can hear me, your little husband bitch is gay. That last so called "business trip" to Baltimore, never happened. Bitch! He was in my ass, right hear in New York." Click . . .

Even at that moment I still loved him. A month after all the calls stopped ; I had run out to the grocery store when the call came in. I couldn't have been gone more than an hour, I know that because when I left Oprah had just started and when I returned she was still on. That's when I saw it, the flashing red light on my answering machine. I was over come by fear; were the calls going to start again? In that hour my life would be changed forever. I carefully neared the machine flashing its red light and pressed play. It was the hospital, "Keith" had been struck by a trailer and was in critical condition. I rushed there to be by his side, like any good wife would. I entered the room to find him bloodied and bruised, tears filled his eyes. He kept telling me how much he loved me and how sorry he was. I was confused. Sorry for what? "You haven't done anything wrong, that man hit you", I said in an effort to calm him. He then said no baby not that, just know that I loved you and I'm sorry. With his last breath those were the final words to leave his lips. I left the room with my arms clenched tightly, tears streaming down my cheeks. His doctor came and rested his hand on my shoulder. "Mrs. Baxter there's no easy way for me to tell you this, I interrupted him. No easy way to tell me what!? That he's dead? I already know that, I did watch him die . . .

"Mrs. Baxter your husband felt it best I tell you. Mrs. Baxter your husband was HIV positive, apparently he's known for a number of months." (Pause) I felt ill. I swallowed hard, remaining speechless. And yet, even at that moment I still loved him. I remember thinking that man had never been sick a day in his life, he never even took as much an aspirin for as much a headache. How could I miss AIDS medication? I know now that in a matter of speaking I was sentenced to death because I was too busy turning my head ; to save myself early on. I loved him. I still love him. My husband, my Keith, my love, my poison.

Signed,
Keith's Wife

It was letters such as these or the accounts as I prefer to call them that have touched me. Stories of hatred, revenge, murder and overwhelming sadness. The words of lovers scorned by those who pledge loyalty to them. These were people not in search of answers but people looking to be heard. Fortunately for me, I was the one they chose to confide in.

I am Doctor Sarah Dillard and twice a month I write for a small Bronx newspaper. In the three years I've been writing for the paper I have read 6,974 letters with questions I was glad to answer as best I professionally could. But of those 6,974 letters only a select few hold a special place in my heart, tucked away in my home and stored with love away from judgmental eyes.

I spent years in school to come to the realization that being a doctor wasn't what I wanted to do. I want to be free spirit, I wanted to be an inspiration to others. It wasn't until recently when I left the newspaper to pursue my own enlightenment that I came to the understanding that before I could achieve this goal; I would have to find the composers of these accounts. Luckily I was successful in contacting them. In speaking with them directly, I also realized their words deserved to be heard by someone other than myself. There are many women and men that could benefit from reading these accounts. It is my hope that in publishing the accounts, others will learn from what has been written.

The accounts are written testaments that treachery comes in all forms, it doesn't discriminate, and the accounts prove that the sex of an individual plays no part in ones capacity to hurt or deceive. These accounts . . . Are they real? Yes they are, as real as you or I? The circumstances in which they are written . . . Fictional? Maybe. But none of this changes the fact that these are fictional truths, realistic possibilities, testaments to what we all have felt, done or wanted to do because of a broken heart. Some may seem extreme but ask yourself; if put in the same position, would I have done the same? Or. Would I have reacted in the same fashion?

These are "The Accounts of the Scorned."
Read and think . . .

Part 1

When violating the moral boundaries of ones relationship we can only expect to cause an unforeseeable amount of damage.

Dear Dr. Dillard,

I am the daughter of a pastor. Born and raised in Flagstaff, Arizona. I met him in my daddy's church. I called him my chocolate dream. I have always been attracted to black men, it's just he's was the first I had ever been with because he was the first not afraid to speak to me. Most guys were afraid of my father. He began picking me up from school, we'd sneak off to his grandmothers house. For the first time in my life I had begun lying to my parents. I'd lie and tell them I was at cheerleading or at choir practice, sometimes I'd claim to be at a friend's house. Because if they found out I was having sex, worse having sex with a black guy. They'd kill me. Well eventually they did find out and tried to separate us. So we did what a lot of kids do. We ran off. Yeh, we went right to Georgia to stay at his auntie house. That was until God stepped in and snatch him from me. After the funeral his auntie put me out. I had no where to go, I was homeless for weeks. I couldn't call my daddy, he disowned me after Jackson and I left. I wanted to die, I even tried to kill myself. That's when I met "Deon', he rescued me. He took me to his home, fed me, he encouraged me to get a job and said I could stay until I get on my feet. At first I was apprehensive but he was real nice to me the way "Jackson" was. We were okay for a while, then he started to complain that I didn't make enough money at my job and how I needed to help out more if I was going to live there. I looked for a new job but pickings were slim because I hadn't finished high school and I didn't have any skills. His suggestion was that I strip. "My home boy got a club, you could dance there. You heard me 34, 26, 42? (He didn't call me by name, he called me by my dimensions). You pretty and you got rhythm, which is rare in you white girls." he said. I'll admit the money was good but he started taxin' me for more money, eventually he'd just take everything I made for the night. He would make me feel like I had owed him for the rest of my life. He wouldn't let me go anywhere by myself. He'd drop me off and pick me from the club. I was a prisoner. When I was in the house he'd rape me and then lock me in a closet in his room, like I was an animal. Sometimes he'd come back angry because he lost all his money (correction, MY money) in a dice game. Those were the worst times because he'd drag me out of the closet rape me, beat me bloody, leave me to tend to my own wounds and still expect me to prepare his dinner. He'd say 34, 26,42 I ain't never letting you go, you worth your weight in gold girl. He gave me Gonorrhea twice, Chlamydia once, Trich, and one time he even gave me crabs. It's 2000 and what? Who still gets crabs? He must have been fucking dogs, hood rat ghetto broads who sleep with 10 guys from Monday to Sunday. And even at this point I still felt like I owed him my life. It wasn't until one night when he brought me home from the club, we were sitting outside in his Chevy when he punched me in face, breaking my jaw. It was at that point I knew I had to get away. I pulled his gun from underneath my seat and began firing shots into his chest until I emptied the clip. I dropped the gun and called the police. I sat beside the body until the police arrived. I won't go into any further detail about that portion of my life. But I'll tell you this much, I now live in the Bronx and I've been reading your column for a few months and it seems like most of the women that write to you are African—American, I just wanted them to hear about what happened to me so that they can see hurt comes in all colors. It's not just black women that endure heartaches.

Signed,
Bruised Georgia Peach

Dear Dr. Dillard,

Does cheating give you a motive to kill? Does a ruined life give you motive to kill? Is hatred really motive for killing? He has no family, I'm his family and he has very few friends. Do you think I could kill him and get away with it? It's not like he'd be missed or anything. He's a jerk. Always stepping on people to get what he wants, he's a liar, a cheater, he carries disease and sickness. He's the perfect example of a disgusting individual. He couldn't keep his dick in his pants if his life depended on it, wearing a condom forget about it. For God sakes, it was okay for people to see us a pair of poor little orphan cousins, which only had each other. At first that is how it was. We grew up like brother and sister. When I was six my mother died so my aunt and uncle took me in and then when I was sixteen they were murder in a robbery. I ended up moving in with "Patrick" my cousin who was twenty-two at the time. He comforted me when I would cry, I took their deaths a lot harder than he did. It was during one of my crying spouts that it happened, we kissed. It was so soft and

3

passionate then it became rough; you know the way kids ripping open their presents at Christmas time. I gave him my virginity; that's where it all began. He'd make love to me every night exploding inside me, I loved him so but I hate him too. He'd make love to me and then go out meet girls and bring them home, where I'd sit in my room listening to him have sex on the same bed we made love in so many times. I went on birth control because he didn't want to use condoms after all I'm not crazy I do know we shouldn't make babies. Behind closed doors we were like a real couple. He'd slap my butt while I served him dinner, he'd sneak into the shower with me, he'd even get jealous when his friends would look at me or if they asked if I was dating anyone. After all I was just his cousin. Right? I was happy but things change. He'd give me S.T. D's and then accuse me of sleeping with his friends but I wouldn't do that Dr. Dillard, I loved him, I lived for him, he protected me, he was my only family, the only one I wanted to share my body with. That being said. Would any of these things constitute murder? Do I deserve to die as well, Dr. Dillard?

Sincerely,
My Only Love

What's goody, Dr. Dillard?

I'm not all that good at writing dear such and such letters. So instead I put this together some parts from my slam book. I'm the type of chick that's kinda rough around the edges, I'm not what you'd call beautiful and everybody around me expects certain shit not to bother me but I still have the same feelings as other woman. Let me know should I leave or stay? And if I do go will I be able to find a new dude? Maybe he treats me the way he does because he knows I don't really want to leave or because no one else will want me? So here we go and after you read it please hit me back and let me know what I should do.

"This nigga set me on fire, he burned me but it wasn't by flame. Got my pussy sneezing and running like water. In my fucking bed, the next bitch that's where I caught her. I probably woulda killed him if it weren't for his daughter. Six years, a big belly and a fake ring. After all this shit I've said I still don't know where to begin. You call yourself a hustler, a man so why am I the one that has to provide for your first baby moms. You're weak I make 50g a year and all your accounts read 1,025 a dime and a quarter. All this and a lot more with your trifling ass I'm still caught up. My lungs weak from all that screaming and fussing, just plain tired of telling you what not to stick ya dick in. I love you with my all but just to see you makes me sick. I promised myself I wouldn't but I started to suck ya dick, I loved you so I'd swallow and refused to spit."

Sincerely,
The Rapstress

Dear Dr. Dillard,

"Shandi if you're hearing this tape you know what I've done. It all became to much for me and I couldn't handle it. I lost everything . . .

Looking at Jordan these past few days has been so hard for me. Knowing what that son of a bitch did to me ate me up inside and that Bitch Val! My own sister, how could she do this to us? Her niece and me her little sister. How could she hurt us like that? He was like a brother to you and Val or at least he should have been after all these years. I don't know what came over me; she looked so much like him. I just, I just . . . (crying)

Every time I looked at her I would see his face and I would start to cry. Then the crying became anger and that last time I became overwhelmed by rage. I started shaking her, Shandi I shook my baby. Shandi her body is so limp in my arms, so small. I extinguish my own child's life. Shandi I need to lay beside my baby. I love you big sis."

That's where the tape ended. My sister cut her wrist. I found the tape on the floor beside the two bodies. My nieces' small body lay there as if she had fallen asleep and just never woke up. My sisters body was encircled by dried blood, there were maggots and flies every where. After over three weeks what else could be expected. That was how long I hadn't heard from my little sister. You see I live in New York but she and Val lived in Florida so I couldn't just pop over to check on her and couldn't send Val for obvious reasons. When I arrived that was the condition in which I found them. During the buzz of the police investigators, coroners and reporters I slipped off to the bedroom, where I listened to the tape. My sister had shaken my niece to death and took her own life once she realized what she did. Some time has past but I get up every morning and listen to that tape. It causes me so much pain to know that my little sister is gone but I take comfort in still being able to hear her voice. Its' a torturous comfort. I no longer speak to my sister Val.

Signed,
Shandi

Dear Dr. Dillard,

This is my second letter to you but it's the first I've actually mailed. I love reading your column, I use to say to myself how do these women let these men get away with the things they do? I now see because I'm now one of those women. I'm now one of the women I used to see on TV, read about in papers and in magazines.

We were co-workers, we'd been shamelessly flirting like school children. I couldn't help it he was fine. You know . . . The type of fine that as soon as he walks into a room you wanna jump his bones. He exudes sex. Just looking at him made me want to be a freak, just fuck! No love making. If you get my drift. Thinking about those times almost makes me forget what he does to me.

We currently live together but not in a way most would understand. I sleep in one room he sleeps in the other. How the hell did that happen!? Okay I'll explain. Originally we agreed we were just having fun, you know friends with benefits, all the perks of a relationship with none of the hassle. We went on this way for about a year until I got pregnant. Wow! Big mistake on my part. I thought him wanting to move in together and wanting to keep the baby was his way of saying lets make it official. Wouldn't you think the same? I got a large two bedroom apartment but instead of making the second bedroom the nursery he turned it into his own lil love nest. He'd flaunt other women in front of me and when they inquired as to who I was he always says "Oh! Her she's my friend don't worry about her she's cool" and then sweep them of to his bedroom. I lost the baby last month but I'm still here hoping he will come to his senses. There has to be some part of him that loves me.

Signed,
Fuck Buddy

Dear Dr. Dillard,

I'm a dirty bitch. I won't deny it, I cant deny it. I hear all these chicks complaining about how they man burned them or cheated or some dumb shit. I'm straight out of Wash. PJ's, lets face it everybody is burning somebody who doesn't cheat? You tell me that. My boyfriend cheats on the regular, when he burns me I go to the clinic get the cure. Then I wait to see how long it takes him to tell me that he caught something and if he doesn't say anything I'll fuck him again, go right back to the same clinic get the cure, go home and curse him out for giving me something. Once he caught the clap from that bitch in 3B and then gave it to me, I had that shit in my throat and my pussy. Double burn. But anyway I left his broke ass alone, after what? Five years. I'm good. But Sarah that's not even why I'm writing. I met this dude and I love him, I mean a lot. He's one of those good dudes, one of them that wants out of the hood. He wants me to go back to school and get all educated and shit. I like that, he's the first dude to care where I end up. He wants to get married and have kids. I could really see myself wit him. But all those years of abusing my pussy has taken its toll. I got herpes and I'm afraid to tell him, I've never been afraid to tell anyone anything in my whole life that's how I know I love him. Then having his babies that's out because my cervix is all so fucked up, I couldn't hold a baby in my womb even if I used my hands. I can't tell him that. I'm mad, mad at my ex for all the bullshit, mad at myself for not being smarter, just mad.

Signed,
Bx Burning

Dear Dr. Dillard,

We were together three years, six months and two days when I told him I wanted more of a commitment. I thought it was time for us to get married he tried to avoid the issues, so I gave him an ultimatum either we make steps towards an engagement or I was gone. He said we'd talk about it when he comes back from his trip, I agreed that was reasonable.

A day before he was supposed to come home I went to his place to straighten up so that when he came back he'd feel at ease when he gets home. To my surprise he was already in New York. I saw him go into his house with a girl. I wasn't going to become Miss Ghetto USA, so I waited until the girl left, then I gave him some time to fall asleep. I used my key to let myself in. I stopped in the kitchen and then made my way towards the bedroom. There he was sprawled out across the bed. I smiled for second and then his house phone rang it was the other woman leaving a message to let him know that she had gotten home safely. I became faint, I blacked out. When I came to my clothing was riddled with blood, I looked over he was dead. Very calmly dragged his body to the bathroom, placed him in the tub and began cleaning. After the house was in order I called out from work and went to the supermarket. I bought groceries for the house and all the ice I could fit in my car. When I returned to his house I packed his body with ice and proceeded to make dinner. I repeated the same ritual each day. I'd pack his body with ice, clean and prepare three square meals a day. We even continued have normal conversations at dinner, well not really normal. I'd ask him a question and then get angry when he wouldn't answer.

After two weeks it all came to an end when she showed up. The other woman. She found us in the bathroom, while we were having dinner and ran from the house screaming. I knew what was going to happen. I leaned on the side of the bathtub and waited. I sat shivering awaiting my faint. The police rushed in, snatching me from the ground. I haven't spoken a word since my arrest. This letter is my first, my last and only attempt at outside communication. There' nothing else to be said . . .

Signed,
Prisoner S6849159

Dear Dr. Dillard,

Some might call me a chicken-head or more commonly a gold digger. I prefer to be referred to as a business woman. I see a way to make a great deal of money and I make it. I've dated doctors, lawyers and businessmen. But it would be a drug dealer that would bring me to my knees. Generally I don't get emotionally involved with the men I date. He was an exception, he had a little bit of everything, he spoiled me like the others but he knew when to tell me no and in all my years of being a business woman no one ever told me no. I learned the inns and outs of the drug game. I fell in love. Like most men once they know that you love them, that's when he starts cheating, sleeping out all the time, taking you for granted and in cases like mine physical abuse. Yes from time to time he saw fit to introduce his fist to my face. I caught a charge for his trifling ass and did six months, with no thanks, no sorry, nothing . . .

He visited me once! On that visit I told him how I felt about the way he treated me. It was on that day I realized men truly aren't worth the ground we walk on. They are the scum of the Earth. His reply was as follows "Fuck you! 'Cause it's clear you really don't know who I am, who I be. You being in jail ain't stopping shit out here, I'm still gonna fuck bitches, I'm still gonna make money and I don't cry. You think you special but you're not. Point blank. I get money, I can buy a million bitches that look like you with half the brains. That's the problem with smart bitches, ya'll ask to many questions. Shut the fuck up sometimes." He walked out that was the last time we spoke. When I got out of jail, it was business as usual back to my doctors and lawyers. I'm not really happy but I'm content.

Signed,
Business Women

Dear Dr. Dillard,

I always prided myself on being his wifey, his first lady, Hilary to his Bill if you must. I was in severe denial about the kind of man he really was and still is. I didn't leave him in the beginning because I didn't want to give his whores the satisfaction of having him. I rather enjoyed the other girls hating me because I was the only one he acknowledged as his wifey, his love. As time went on I grew and got over that, it was no longer amusing. As our relationship dragged on I came to see I loved that I did love, that much was true but I was no longer in love with him and yet somehow his cheating still hurt me. I finally left him, thanks to myspace. A mutual friend contacted me and directed me to a specific myspace pages. There it was for millions of eyes to see. He was professing his love for numerous other women all of which claimed him as their own, just as I had done. I felt stupid. But that's not what hurt the most it was that I was the one plastered all over his page labeled his wife. The pictures of me in his album read "My Wife" on display for millions of myspace visitors to see. They weren't saying ' oh how cute, he must love her" what they were really saying is "she must be really dumb because just I saw that same man on another page telling another girl how much he loves her too." He broke me, he destroyed my spirit. So I'm left still hurting . . .

Signed,
Hilary

Dear Dr. Dillard,

I read that book Push for the first time a week ago. It was given to me by a friend who thought I would identify with it and I did, some what. It was very similar to my own life. My grandparents raised me after my father died when I was five and from that time I can't remember a night when my grandfather didn't creep into my bedroom. For a few years it was just touching. By age fifteen it became more, he'd force me to perform oral sex on him and then it became completely sexual. Four to five times a week he'd force me to have sex with him. He became like a crazed boyfriend or obsessed lover. Marching me home from school, accusing me of having boyfriends. Sometimes just to get off he'd make up lies about my behavior and then tell my grandmother he was going to dispense his punishment in the basement. Once down stairs he'd strip me naked, bend me over, rape and then beat me with an extension cord. My grandmother would hear my screams and never once came to my aid. He impregnated me. I was carrying my grandfathers' child. I told my grandmother what he had done and she started yelling and screaming telling me that I shouldn't tell such lies and that I was a whore. That night she and my grandfather beat me unconscious and I ended up in the hospital. I told social services my story and they believed me; finally someone believed me.

After the baby was born the DNA test proved my grandfather to be the father. In the courtroom at his sentencing my grandmother had a stroke. I gave the baby up for adoption. Today I am studying to become a social worker so that what happened to me doesn't happen to other children. My grandfather is serving time and my grandmother is in a home. I still see a psychiatrist twice a week.

Signed,
Ms. Push
Dear Dr. Dillard,

I fucked an Arab that's what I told my friends. I had to brag because it wasn't what I expected, people always talk about brothers packing but Amir he didn't just rock my world he flipped it smacked it and rubbed that shit down. I never saw us going any further than sex, lets face it he'd never take me home to mama or so that's what everyone told me. Surprisingly enough he took me to meet her and all hell broke loose. She hated me, not because I'm a half breed (black and Hindi) but it was because I wasn't Saudi and not a Muslim. I thought that day would've been the end of our relationship, it wasn't. He said to hell with his mother and we were later married in quaint ceremony with my family and his closest friends. I was his princess and we were a fairytale couple. That was until the birth of our second son and a few months after 9/11. Amir constantly had run inn's with people on the street calling him a terrorist, telling him to go back to his country, he became increasingly frustrated with what the world had become. He started attending what he called meetings for Muslim pride. His mothers' arrival just added fuel to the fire. She claimed that she was sorry for being foolish and she said she wanted to be involved in the lives of only grandsons. The unions of her other three children yielded seven girls. I had no problem with her being involved with the boys she was the one that had the problem.

By the birth of our third son his entire family had moved back to their country. Amir was a shell of his former self. Always preaching, praying and complaining about how corrupt and racist a country America is. We argued constantly about me not bending to his Muslim extremist views. Then he started this talk about taking the boy to see his mother. I don't know how but he convinced me to let him take little Amir and Kalif to see his mother. Omar stayed with me, he was to young to make the trip. They were only supposed to stay the summer. That was three years ago. I've made and continue to make efforts to find my boys but it's hard to pin point their location. I believe Amir has connections to Al-Qaeda. About once a year he sends me pictures of the boys and a letter. The letter always says the same thing "I still love you, I love Omar I miss you both immensely and I'm sorry you won't see the right in what our people are trying to do, I wish that you would see how wrong America is, little Amir and Kalif are well as you've seen they are thriving." He sent me pictures of them at what looked like one of those training camps you see on television, guns in hand.

Signed,
The Arabian Princess

Dear Dr. Dillard,

My brother was never really good with rejection, to be quite frank he didn't deal very well with much of anything. You see doc after my fathers death my brother suffered a psychotic break and for the past couple of years after his release from the hospital it was my job to keep my brother life stress free, so when he met "Connie" my job was made easier. He was the happiest I had seen him in a long time. He was even making plans for his future and he never talked about having a future. There were a lot of rumors swarming around about Connie though. Rumors about her sleeping around. I wanted to tell him but I didn't know how to tell him. I'd hint here and there about the things I heard but he was so in love with that girl. She had him under her spell and there was nothing I could do to make him see the truth. He'd have to see who she really was on his own. Too bad it would end tragically.

Connie was sleeping with my brothers' best friend and my brother found out. He called me from his apartment, where he had them hostage. He was crying frantically, he told me the police were outside and he wasn't coming out because there was to much for him to do, he had to punish them for what they'd done to him. While talking to me he was dowsing the apartment with lighter fluid.

When I got there the street was filled with people. I stayed on the phone pleading with my brother, then the first shot went off, many dove to the ground, others fled in fear. Then the second shot went off and flames could be seen coming form the window. I remember thinking "Oh my God he shot them" and then my brother appeared in the apartment window amongst the smoke, the phone pressed against his ear. I could hear that he was still crying. He leaped through the window.

When the fire was finally put out, Connie and Anthony's bodies were found bound to the dinning room table and the newspapers painted my brother as a deranged stalker that killed a loving young couple. But the truth is he was an innocent he just chose the wrong girl.

Signed,
Fire Bugs Sister

Dear Dr. Dillard,

I'm sure you've seen those computer match making sites that you see advertised on television or on the trains and buses? Well that's where I met my guy. We liked the same things, he had good job (very important), he was sweet, charming and a freak in the sheets. Although there were some things I had to get use to, though I sometimes questioned them. We were happy, almost like we were made for each other. There was never any drama; no mysterious phone calls, no public confrontations with women most important he never gave me any diseases. Point blank I never had to put up with any of the shit you usually have to deal with when your involved with black or Hispanic men. After about a year or so we got married, we didn't have a honeymoon because we spent a ridiculous amount of money on the wedding and we're both working class people. By the next day we were both back at work. Two days after the wedding I left work early so that I could surprise him with a romantic evening. When I got home I was unpleasantly surprised. I found my groom, my new husband in the living room. In my living room! In our living room! In the 69 position. Eating ass! Eating another mans ass. While the other guy was sucking his dick! He was eating ass Dr. Dillard and getting his dick sucked! It was no wonder I didn't have problems with women he was busy fucking men. The bastard liked men. When you hear moaning coming from your living room as enter your front door, the first thing that comes to mind is my man is fuck another women in my house. Right? But my husband wasn't screwing a skinny little nineteen year old girl he was fucking a big brawny black man. I was pissed, not sad or hurt just pissed!

I got my trusty bat and started swinging on their nasty asses. I chased their naked asses out of my apartment. Then I called 911 and told them the two naked men were having sex in the stairway. Ha! Ha! Ha! I still laugh about that; then I come crashing back down to the reality of the situation. It's bad enough having your man cheat on you with a woman but to cheat on you with a man . . . That broke me down, that took me out the game.

Signed,
Fag Hag Dear

Dr. Dillard,

Baby girl how old are you? You can't be but thirty. Hell, you might be younger than that. Let me tell you something I am 64 years old, I come from a different time than you all. In my day when people got married they stayed married even when they hated each because that was the right thing to do. Those marriages are what you see lasting 30 and 40 years, hell some have lasted a lot longer than that. The problem with you young girls is that you are expecting to much from these men. You wanna be in love, you want unconditional love, well let me tell you some thing else cheating counts as a condition. So stop complaining. My man cheated, he did this he did that. My husband was a low down dirty

17

dog but he provided for our family. Sundays, he kicked my ass religiously and went upside my head like clock work. I tell you what though our marriage remained strong. But you young girls today giving up the draws to men that can't tell you your last name, much less marry you. Having babies with no ring on ya fingers. Like I said before my Albert was a dog and we were married up until his death 20 years ago. With a lot of property and nice chunk of change in the bank. Had being the key word . . .

That young boy must have smelt my money from a mile away. I know I have no business with a 30 year old boy but shit even an old bird needs the occasional back adjustment. The companionship was nice too. I treated that young boy damn good and he cleaned out my bank account. I handled his ass old school I had my sons and a couple of my grand babies track him down and walk his ass. I didn't get my money though. That being said, all that shit I was talking before was crap. Sometimes when your old and you think you know it all. It takes the young to come and teach you something new. I finally felt what you young girls are going through, I think when you start to complain about your man you've finally reached your breaking point. It just took me a while to understand. I hope I'm making some sense.

Signed,
The Cougar

Dear Dr. Dillard,

Have you ever loved so hard that you felt it might crush you? But you're willing to endure it for reasons only your heart could explain. Your brain questioning does he really love me. But your body yearned for the sweet agony he provides. Leaving you torn. This is how it's been since the first day. There are times when he makes me smile, while enjoying our closeness, but those times are so bitter sweet. I would start out so elated but then the faces of his many women would pop into my head and I'd come crashing back to Earth. If he is to kiss me at that very moment, that kiss becomes an argument that envelopes the room and destroys the days peace.

I don't want this any more but my heart, it still clings. Driving me to work harder to make him the man that I deserve. I don't want him, but I do want him. I am willing to take a bullet for him but each time I visit the doctor I realize that he freely jeopardizes my life. Then I sit back and think I am willing to die for him but am I willing to die because of him? He hurts my heart so often and so badly that I have been unable to heal. I know these things but I still linger. I know the type of man he is and I know that I'm down in a ditch that he's dug for the both of us. But I can't leave. I'm just . . . Stuck . . .

Signed,
Kerry

Part 2

A relationship built on deceit, can only end in deceit.

Dear Dr. Dillard,

I don't know which is one is crazier. Being a stalker or stalking your stalker. That's what happened with me. My boyfriend at the time was cheating on me with a crazy women, she started stalking me. She'd call my cell phone thirty times a day and all hours of the night. I'd see her standing outside watching my house long after he'd left, she'd follow me to work. The last straw came when she broke into my house and stole my beautiful African gray. I know it was her because she called me and said she had my baby and then she let me hear him saying who's mommy's baby. A few days later I got a FedEx package with his body in it. The police are like no help. It was my turn now, I flipped the script on her. I started following her around, calling her in the middle of the night and when the time was right my friend and I beat her ass. Even then she didn't stop. She started leaving voice mails on my phone saying she was going to kill me. I filed yet another police report. I gave him a choice he could either give up the three years we had or he could handle his crazy mistress. He kicked her to the curb, he told he to leave us alone, he didn't want her especially considering that when they started the little

20

affair he told her it could never be serious because he already had me. For about a month after that life went back to normal, life was quiet again.

My life was destroyed on September 18, 2005. She followed me on my way to work. She shot me and covered my body in acid. I dragged myself to the corner of 214 and Laconia, where I laid until a woman passing by helped me by calling 911. I was rushed to Jacobi Hospital. Coincidentally it was in Jacobi's ER that she was arrested. Since she burned her hands; they linked her injuries to my assault, I just had to identify her. My face is completely intact but from the neck down I'm a monster. I hate her, I'd have to be a saint not to. I hate him more though because if it wasn't for him I would never have been exposed to her in the first place.

Signed,
Acid Monster

Dear Dr. Dillard,

God inspires us, he tests us but he never gives us more than we can handle. He is all knowing, so he knows the destructive things we are capable of and yet he allows us free will. It is this that makes him divine. It is in his arms that we take comfort. Speaking as a former priest I can no longer be the voice of God. I can't say he protects us because he's never protected me. I can say he has inspired me, just the thought of him awakens a hate inside of me. Oh! Before I forget the part about him never giving you more than you can handle. All a sham. All knowing, he knew a crack addict was going to break into the church and sodomize me and he knew I couldn't handle it but he still allowed it. Was that because the Lord almighty loved me. No! The fact of the matter is that he doesn't care about us and his devoted followers want so much to believe in something that they are to afraid to admit that he's selfish. To afraid to admit that he is sitting up there on his opulent thrown laughing and moving us around like pawns on a Chess board.

Oddly enough it was a similar experience during my younger years that lead me to the priesthood. As an usher I was molested by a priest at my church. After that I vowed one day with Gods help I would be vocal in eradicating this plight from the church. As a priest I would look around, seeing how troubled the world was and continued to believe in him. It wasn't until that night with the crack addicted that I stopped believing. I am no longer one of his foolish lambs.

Signed,
Why father?

Hi Dr. Dillard,

I need somebody to talk to. There is no one for me to talk too. I was sad one day and my mom said she didn't have time to talk to me and she handed me the paper and said maybe she has time to listen to your problems. And now I read your paper all the time. I read it over and over for two weeks until the new one comes out. I read that this is your last month your going to be writing and I don't know what I'm going to do without you. I see that a lot of the people that write to you are women with funny names, well I don't think there names at all. I just wanted to tell you that in case you don't know that those aren't real names. I'm woman too so maybe before you leave the paper you can read about me too.

I want to tell you what happened to me. I told my mom but she didn't believe me she never listens to me because she is always to busy.

Everyday after program me and my friend go to the supermarket to buy chicken because they make the best chicken. But one day she didn't com to program so I had to go by myself. That's was the day a boy that works at the supermarket said he's been watching me and he likes me and he said he had a gift for me in the back. When we got in the back he grabbed me and pushed me on the floor, he hurt me down there. When he stopped he told me to pull up my panties and go. I told him that I was going to tell on him and he said that no one would believe a retard. When I got home my mother wasn't there yet. I had blood in my panty's so I took a shower and when my mom got home I told her what happened and I showed her my panty's and she didn't believe me. She said only bad girls make up lies and the blood is from my period. But I know my period I'm not the smartest girl in the world but I know my period. I know why those other people write to you, it's because they're mad at other people. I'm mad at my mom because she didn't save me from that boy and she never listens to me, she never believes me and she always calls me a burden. Thank you Dr. Dillard for listening to me and I hope you write back.

Signed,
My mom doesn't believe me

Dear Dr. Dillard,

Currently I'm at the 24 hour laundry mat. This is where I come to get away from him. I read your column and find that it's so easy for your other reader to express themselves, it's so easy for them to open up to you. Sitting here the only thing I could think to say is my life is like a double load of laundry at the laundry mat. From the outside it's brightly lit and inviting but once your inside you realize it's just another place to wash away your dirt. I sit in the laundry mat watching my sheets in the spin cycle and wish it would never stop. Because when it does that means I am few minutes closer to having to go home. I love my husband and I know he is one of very few good men but I've come not to hate him but resent him for things I know aren't in his control. Sometimes I have to wonder, is love really enough? My husband has fertility issues so we can't have children. He can't give me a child. As long as I'm with him I'll never know motherhood. I stay because I love him and I dare not cheat, but I stay. I'm just sitting here watching the double load machine wash away the seeds that will never bare fruit, painful reminder that I will remain childless and forever will be. Sperm donors, adoption he won't hear of it. He said either he's the one to get me pregnant or it's not happening which means it will never happen. Well Dr. Dillard I have to get back to my sheets. I'll write again.

Signed,
Double Load

Dear Dr. Dillard,

I am . . . Excuse me. I was a 34year old virgin up until three weeks ago. I'm not want you would call classically beautiful in fact I'm not even slightly cute. I've been called Magilla Gorilla, Ug Mug and any name you can think of to refer to ugly people. I've gone through life avoiding men because most of them are out of my league even the sleazy ones. To make matters worse I'm not the sharpest tool in the shed. I got lucky in the money department though. My dad is similar to a real life George Jefferson he owns 23 laundry mats all over the U.S. Thank God for that. I'm a trust fund baby.

Now that I've given you little bit of my background, I am now ready to share with you my secret shame.

I love oral sex, I want to have sex but I can't find a guy that wants to be with me and I'm not about to give my virginity to someone that I don't love. Where as a blow job can be done casually, or at least that is my belief. I like the way my lips felt around a mans' shaft. No man will ever refuse a blowjob so that's always been my way of being close with a man. No man has ever stepped up and said he wanted me as his girlfriend, I'm not pretty; at all! If your starving and there's no food anywhere, if someone was to hand you shit on a plate you're going to take it, eat it and love it. That's how I live. If sucking a few cocks will buy me time with a man, any man I'm game.

I got mixed up with one of my fathers customers. For the first time in 34years I thought I finally found some one who was willing to look past my physical short comings. Someone who wanted to be with me because of what's on the inside. He was so charming. If you need to ask . . . Yes! I did suck his cock too. In fact I think it was my best work ever, I had him calling my name every time his tip hit the back of my throat. His toes curled as he grasped my head in ecstasy. We started spending more and more time together. He wore a lot cheap clothing, so I did what Beyonce did and upgraded him. Manicures, Gucci shoes and shades. You name it he now had it. I was head over heels for him and ready to let go of my virginity.

He made the arrangements. We ate a Tavern on the Green (I paid), went on a carriage ride in the park and we retired back to the Bronx. He paid for a motel. Yuck! My first time was going to be in a shady Bronx motel. I regret not demanding to stay in Manhattan. To my surprise the place was very clean. As soon as we took off our coats, he instructed me to take off my clothing. He kissed my neck softly as he guided me towards the bed and asked if I was ready. I said yes. He laid me on the bed, then tied my hands to the bed post and placed the silk tie I had bought him into my mouth. He said don't worry I'm just putting the tie in your mouth because I know you're going to scream and the sound of a woman screaming makes my dick soft. I didn't resist it because I trusted him. He got up from the bed. I could see the bathroom door open, three men walked out. The room exploded with laughter. Fear over took me. I couldn't scream, I couldn't move. One guy said "Yo doggs, you're right she is an ugly thing. For real!" Marlon replied "Yeh she's ugly but I know that pussy is tighter than two fat men fighting in a phone booth." Their laughter grew louder. I was the butt of his jokes. Marlon placed a pigs mask over my face and said "lets go boys I'm ready to hear this piggy squeal." They took turns with me for four hours straight. Mercilessly pounding my small opening. When they were done, they left me there humiliated for the cleaning crew to find. I'll leave it at that for now because at this time I am unable to discuss the legal proceedings against Marlon and his friends.

Signed,
Virginia

Dear Dr. Dillard,

She was breath takingly beautiful. Her eyes were so dark and deep like pools of oil, it seemed like I'd be lost forever. And for a time I was lost in her. She was perfection to me. Her lips were soft and always sweet. It wasn't just her physical beauty that kept me though, it was her mind. She was so clever, so witty, her mind spoke volumes for some one of such few years. We met while I was on assignment with my husband in Uganda.

She was a student. Before that day I had never felt any sexual attraction to a woman, in fact I had never been with anyone other than my husband of four years. In that first engaging conversation I knew that I could spend the remainder of my life with her and I thought I would. When I returned to the U.S it would be a year before I would see her again. But in that year we engaged in secret correspondences like forbidden lovers do in the romance novels. When she finally returned to the U.S we were together once again. After months of cheating; I could no longer continue to lie and deceive a man that for so many years I called my heart.

One night I sat him down and told him everything. Tears spilled down his face I could feel his heart withering. At the time I felt terrible about the situation but I soon felt at ease, I was now free to love the woman I lived for. The night I told her I left Steven, I planned the perfect dinner. I hired a personal chef and two servers. We ate, we laughed and at the end of the night I told her I had left Steven. The smile on her face faded. She said to me "You should go back to your husband, we were just having fun and it would never be more than that. I thought you knew that!" she also told me that she was engaged to the son of a prominent Ugandan barrister. She said goodbye, kissed my forehead and walked out of my life. That was it. I was crushed . . .

I did go back to Steven and he welcomed me back with open arms. Every time Steven touches me I shutter because it isn't her touch. I think of her often, Steven knows this. We both know that some things are best left the way they are.

Signed,
Heartbroken

Dear Dr. Dillard,

All my life I've had bad luck especially with men.
I have a crush on this guy and I'm to old to still have
crushes and even if I had the capacity to engage the
opposite sex, I've been screwed up by the things that
have happened to me throughout miserable existence.

The first incidents that I can remember were from
when I was small. My mothers' boyfriend molested me.
They were both professional junkies. While in one of her
drug induced states my mother watched as her boyfriend
sodomized repeatedly. When they were really hard up
for cash he'd allow his friends to rape me in exchange for
money to feed their habit. Children's Services stepped in
and placed me in a foster home until they could track
down my grandparents.

Age twelve was when I was placed in the home of a
seemingly pleasant couple. It was great for a while. Then
the husband started in on me. He'd rape me during the
night while his wife was asleep. He was really sick, he'd
pull my hair, lick my face and making growling sounds
in my ear. Sometimes he'd pretend he was an overseer
and I was a slave girl and he'd make me say "no Massa,
I's a good girl." That's how he got his rocks off. I felt the
way I did when I lived with my mother. His wife had
become suspicious and one night she didn't go to sleep.
She caught him in the act. I was crying and the bed
was soaked with ejaculate. She pulled me from the bed
and told him to get out. Then she called the police and
my social worker. She apologized to me and asked me
to stay. I did stay but only until my grandparents were
found. And when they were I moved in with them. Life
was great with them, it was near perfect. When it was
time to further my education they paid for the school of
my choice. They'd send care packages once a week and
called everyday. During my junior year my grandfather

past; that was the year I met with another of my tragic run inn's with men. While on my way back to my dorm from the library two men dragged me in to a dark van and drove me to a remote location. They brutally raped me. One of the masked men tried to force me to perform oral sex on him and for the first time in my life I decided to stand up for myself. I took his penis into my mouth and bit down as hard as I possibly could. I felt his blood spilling down my face, he was screaming in pain. The other man struck me in the back of my head. I released the hold my teeth had on his penis, he keeled over and his partner started beating me with his crowbar. They pulled off and pushed me from the moving van. I laid at the side of a desolate road hoping that God would end my suffering and let me die. I awoke nearly a week later with my grandmother at my bedside. I think I go through so much now because maybe in a previous life I was evil, a tyrant or something. All I can do is heal and hope nothing else happens to me.

Signed,
UnluckyDear

Dr. Dillard,

Are you familiar with the Jamaican way of thinking. You should be everyone is. If you're not, Jamaicans are very homophobic, which makes my life more complicated because I'm both Jamaican and gay. I live in a predominantly Jamaican neighborhood. I live on White Plains Rd. in the Bronx and I work and play in the city. I moved to the U.S 12years ago. Generally I stay far from people in my neighborhood but given the proper incentives anyone can be persuaded to change their views. It was the craziest thing. I started getting flower and chocolate deliveries to my apartment from a mystery admirer. Then there were gift baskets, Visa gift cards; those were my favorites. The first gift card he sent was folded in a note that said:

"To my future boo, I want you to wear the best no more H& M.
Your secret lover"

At about 7o'clock one evening I finally caught him leaving one of his gifts. Oh! My God! He looked so nice. He looked like a real "bad man" rough and bandy legged and he was a drug dealer. I was in love instantly. We went away on the weekends, he took me shopping and made love to me yard style. He use to kiss my forehead and tell me he loved me. We couldn't make any real movement around the Bronx but that's a small price to pay for happiness.

When his friends told him about the rumors about me and him, he denied me. He stopped coming to see me. He'd call me and tell me he can't over because "im nuh (he didn't want) want 'im(his) woman an 'im frens dem fi find out 'bout we (about us)". I understand where he was coming from at first but when him and his friends broke into my apartment it was too much. They beat me up, dem piss pon mi (on me), dem (they) pour bleach pon ni clothes, mash up mi T.V an speakers. I couldn't file a police report because the laws of ghetto life forbid it. One minute he was pledging his love for me the next he was nearly killing me. Mi nah hide weh mi is. Unuh Jamaican bad man weh love fuck batty need fi stop say bun batty man 'cau unuh a batty man too. (Loosely translated: I'm not ashamed of who I am. You Jamaican tough guys or gangsters need to stop condemning gays because many of you are gay yourselves.)

Signed,
Fassy

30

Dear Dr. Dillard,

I am a 19 year old collegian and now days a girls my age are no longer be virgins. Some even younger than myself already have children. I have a longing to be a in a relationship, a longing to be some ones girlfriend and I think it's high time for me to lose my virginity. I want to know what all the hype is about. But then I stop and think . . . Do I really want these things? Do I want the trouble that comes with being in a relationship with a man. My family thinks I a lesbian. But little do they know that my reasons for not having a boyfriend rests in the hands of the males in my family.

I see what they do to the woman they supposedly to love. First there's my father every chance he gets he's cheating on my mom and on numerous occasions I watched him beat her as if she were a beast of burden. And I hate him for that. In turn I hate men because my father is a man. My brothers, well they're young but I already see that the roads ahead of them will be paved with broken hearts. Next there's my cousin "Tom" his girlfriend just gave birth to his first child (another boy to add the family) and his girl on the side is due to give birth to his second child in a week. I feel for her because she doesn't even know and once she finds out, she will be crushed. I hate him for this wrong and I hate men because my cousin "Tom" is a man. My third example is of my other cousin "Mark", he has a fiancé who is well read, pretty and she was there for him when he only made 250 dollars a week; even when he was without a job and made nothing. And, what did he do? He destroyed their relationship with infidelity. Cheating on her with senseless scallywags, when he was down and out she stayed, those girls disappeared a long with his money. I hate him too. So I hate men because my cousin "Mark" is a man.

If relationships that aren't my own scare me in such a way, what can I expect in my future? Would the same scenarios play out in my relationships? If the opposite of love is indifference; would what I think is love really be hate? If so what kind of love life is that to have? Or is that how love is suppose to be? I've also been thinking about another possibility; it is said that the sins of the father shall be visited upon his children, if this is the case I will never be happy because men with treat me or try to treat me the way my father has treated woman. This means either way I'm doomed.

Signed,
Doomed

Dear Dr. Dillard,

Have any of your patients been substance abusers? My story is one of a good girl gown bad. I was always a straight laced kid. I remained that way long after we met. To tell you the truth when I first met him I couldn't stand him. We both attended well known art high school. He was the angry loner, obsessed with painting about the darkness of human suffering and I was the popular afro-centric type involved in all school activities. Every chance he got he'd bother me, all we could do was argue. As fate would have it our econ teacher forced us to work together on a class project. By the third day of the project I knew that I wanted to be with him but some how he knew we were destined (I love that word "destined") even before I myself realized it. Moving along . . .

Here I am today. It's been a month since he overdosed. We both did tried to overdose, I lived. It wasn't suppose to turn out that way but I lived. There was a time when I was the only one clean. I'd smoke pot from time to time though. He got me to try the heroine, he told me it was like have sex flowing through your veins. When he was high it was like he was in different place, he was so creative, it was that creativity that paid for our Manhattan loft and helped put me through college. I started shooting up with him, I wanted to be creative too, I wanted to be the new "It girl" of the art world, I didn't want to be known a "Matt's" black girlfriend. When we had the habit under control it was great. But bad times hit, the heroine stopped doing it's job, it ceased to continue inspiring him. With increased failure to produce art, the need for the drug became greater. Gallery owners no longer wanted to deal with his volatile moods, the money dwindled, the people we thought were friends abandoned us and finally we lost the loft.

We ended up living in Hunts Point in the Bronx. We were at the lowest point in our lives, his habit worsened and I followed right behind him. Of course the quality of the product was low grade but it had to suffice. We both started prostituting. It's amazing what you will do for the drug. Drugs made a beautiful and artistic man into a fiend giving blow jobs for a fix. I myself a college grad doing the same. When we couldn't make enough to feed the habit, we resorted to stealing from our families. This was to much to handle, we were ready to let go let of this life. We made a pact to die together, only it didn't work out the way we had planned. He died, I lived. Why? I wake up everyday hating myself; sometimes for not dying and other times for not fighting for the both of us, not demanding we seek help. There are days when I wake up crying, cursing his name. Why did he have to make me love him!? Why for eight years did he make me depend on him always to be there for me? Why did he have to leave me? Why did he have to leave us? I should have been all the inspiration he needed. Why wasn't I his inspiration? I look down at my growing belly and say to it "perhaps had he known about you, you the little baby that I carry inside of me. Had we found out about you before we made the pact, things would be different." Dr. Dillard maybe he/ she could have been his reason for living. His inspiration.

Signed,
The Starving Artist

Part 3

As human beings we sometimes pervert the purist of Gods gifts. Drunk with our own insecurities we make foolish decisions. We make the choice to create a life merely to cling something that no longer exists. A child in no way ensures that the relationship you struggle to hold on to will survive.

Dear Dr. Dillard,

Every little girl dreams about their wedding day. I have been dreaming and planning my wedding since I was ten. When "Washington" proposed I knew my vision of the perfect wedding would come true and since it is rare to see black folks getting married in the Bronx, it was important for my wedding to be B.B.P (big, beautiful and perfect). My parents paid for the wedding his parents paid for the reception, we didn't have to come out of pocket for anything. After almost a year of planning, our day came.

I was so nervous, not wedding jitters nervous it was more like impending doom nervous. I felt sick like something was wrong. I walked back and forth between the chapel where our guest awaited us and my dressing room. My groom hadn't arrived yet. Something was wrong and there was nothing I could do to change it. I went to the chapel for the 5th time in an hour but this time something or someone caught my eye. There was a young girl sitting in the last pew on the grooms side, her face stirred me, I once again felt sick, my heart stopped pumping blood and started to pump fear. I felt light headed thinking about her face. I sat for a moment to compose myself and then I heard music, it was time for my wedding march. I made my way up the isle toward my groom. This wasn't what I had pictured for my wedding day, he didn't have on his suit, his clothing was disheveled, he looked hung over. I was upset but the wedding had to go on, this was my dream.

Standing in front my groom I was overcome with joy but that strange fear still loomed over my head. The ceremony was going beautifully until we got to the part where the priest said "If there is anyone here that feel these two should not be wed, speak now or forever hold your piece". Remember the girl I mentioned earlier in this letter, well she stood up. The whole church turned to see her. My groom grabbed my hands tightly and spoke up. He said "No she doesn't have anything to say" the church refocused their attentions on us. He continued to speak. "Baby I love you that's why I asked you to marry me and it is because I love you I can't lie to you. Last night at my bachelor party I met Kandy, the girl you see standing. I think I might be in love with her too and I owe it to myself to see to explore the possibility that it might be more than a fling." He' kissed me, ran to the end of the isle, grabbed her hand and ran out of the church. My heart shattered, I crumbled to the floor. I take that back I shattered.

Signed,
Glass BrideDear

Dr. Dillard,

I'm a statistic. He took advantage of my youth and made me a statistic. I've been told that when you're young you make mistakes because of inexperience and you are to learn from those mistakes. A mistake should make you smarter. Not in my case I think I used my youth as an excuse to be stupid. At age sixteen I had my first daughter with a 27 year old man. This was a 27 year old man with nothing to offer me but a stiff dirty dick. He has no money, no education and he sleeps with anything in a skirt and I mean anything. If it wasn't for my mom and dad he'd be homeless. We lived in their house, ate their food and they put clothes on our daughters back. My parents worked, I dropped out of school so I could work. He sat around the house doing nothing he wouldn't even lift his hand to clean. I overlooked his laziness because I liked the fact that we were a family. He eventually got tired of hearing my parents calling him a bum. He moved into a rented room and urged me to quit my job and move in with him. I did, like a ding bat. Instead of getting a job like a real man would, he forced me to go on welfare so I could stay home and take care of the baby and pay the rent on his furnish room, sorry "our furnished room". I feel so stupid telling you these things but I can't talk to my friends because none of them have children and they don't have time because there planning their senior trips and getting ready for prom. I'm pregnant again and when I told him he was happy, he even seemed more excited than he was when I had our first daughter. I wasn't because we had no money and we could barely take care of the one we had. He assured me that he was going to be a better man and he also said he was going to get a job. I kept the baby because I believed in him because that's what you do when you love someone and you think that person loves you back. In my second trimester he packed up and left while I was asleep. He ran off with my aunt. He left a note that said he never really loved me, he only stayed with me because I got pregnant and now that I'm pregnant with the second baby he realizes he doesn't want to be a father at all and he wishes me luck in the future. I let a man mold me in to the stereotypical idea of a black woman.

Signed,
All AloneDear

Dr. Dillard,

My baby moms bought me a copy of your paper, she said I should write to you because she thinks I'm depressed. That's some crazy shit a man that's depressed. Yeah right! Don't get me wrong some times I think she might be right, that's if it's possible. I mean there are doctors in here I could talk to but how do I look requesting to speak with one of them, voluntarily going to see them. Niggas in here will start to think I'm soft then I'm gonna have problems on my hands. I've done a pretty good job at keeping niggas away from my ass and I want to keep it that way. That's why I'm writing to you.

I want to tell you about my baby moms, she's the one I told you brought me the paper. Yo she's like a real down chick. See she is the first of my five baby mamas. She was there for me the first time I got locked up, she was there when I had babies with those other chicks, she was just there for me point blank. She's still here for me, she's the only one of my baby mamas that comes to see me. This is my second bid and she comes up here once a month for the past two years. She's that good to me and I've never been even close to treating her like that. I can't tell you it doesn't hurt me to see her cry because of the things I've done to her or cry because I make her worry about me. Because the truth is hurts me but I can't help but do it.

I've had mad time to read and I've been reading a lot about the human mind and psychology and I figure if this was a real session, you'd be telling me I got issues with my mother. If you're asking. I might say yes. I love my mom even though she's never really been there for me. A mother is nothing like a father. You don't really expect you're father to be there for you when you need him, 'cause fathers are never really there, even when they live with you. My pop was in jail my whole life. He wasn't there and the older I got I thought my mom would want to be there for me even more, you know play both roles (play mother and father). She wasn't, she was always out doing her. I need help with home work she'd tell me to ask my teacher about it when I got to school, she never cooked for me. If I wanted to eat I had to cook for myself or go next door to the neighbors. Once a week I had to steal money from her purse to buy food for the house. I washed my own clothes, I did all the things she as a mother should have been doing for me. When I got in trouble that was the only time she'd speak to me. She'd curse me and tell me I was no good and how I'd never amount to anything, just like my daddy. I'd still get into trouble just to hear her speak to me. Negative attention is better than no attention, right? She was a drunk but is that any reason for not being a mother? I'm not blaming her for my current situation, this is my fault. It's not her fault I'm in the Bing every other month, that's on me. I'm a criminal because of me. But when it comes to my baby mom the reason I can't give her the love that she needs is because my mom never showed me love and she never taught me how to express love. I don't know how to love the one person in the world that gives a fuck about me. Tell my mom I hate her.

Signed,
The Kid Dear

Dr. Dillard,

Do what you will with this letter. Send it to all your friends make it the butt of all the jokes at your little social events, I don't care what you do with it. I deserved it for doing the things I've done to my fellow woman. I've slept with men that had wives, fiancés and girlfriends. I had no qualms about doing it. What those men weren't getting at home I was glad to give, I did the nasty things those wives, fiancés and goody to shoe girlfriends wouldn't do. Everything I did with those men had a stigma attached to it but I was willing to do it because I expected it remain within the confines of my bedroom.

One of the men I was sleeping with liked to tape our times together, I didn't care because if those tapes were leaked his relationship was at risk and my reputation with the public would be soiled. Out of all the men I've ever slept with he had it the best, there were night of golden showers, tossed salads, I drank his babies and every now an then I'd let him give me a chocolate shower. All on tape. Most of the time it was easy for me to separate my feelings from the sex but he treated me differently from the other men he gave me things and made me smile. Eventually I grew to love him and I waged war on his girl friend. I wanted to be with him, I didn't want to share him with another woman even if she was there before me. I wanted him. He didn't like this at all. He threaten to release the tapes of us, I called his bluff and told him to do it because if he did his woman would leave him.

What I didn't know was that he had already told her about the tapes. He and his friends made DVD's of the most degrading parts of those tapes and dispersed them through out the neighborhood. Everyone now knew what I was doing behind closed doors. I had to move because I was to embarrassed to show my face in front of the people I would see everyday. I thought he cared for me but he was just using me to get what he wanted. He's still in the neighborhood like he's some fucking king with a dick made of gold or something and I live in exile in a neighborhood I don't know. I wish I could see him on the street and spit in his face. But to be real if I had the chance it probably pass me by, that situation had made me into a punk. I was once head strong but now I'm soft and walk with my head down.

Signed,
Living in Exile

Dear Dr. Dillard,

He had a split tongue like the serpent in the Garden of Eden. His words were sweetly venomous. To my body his touch was warm and sensual, to my soul his touch was sickening. All that I believed to be true was tainted and abandoned at his word. The meaningless volumes he spoke couldn't fill a thimble but they crept into my ears and were able to fill my head.

"Abandon your false God, your Jesus and paradise shall be set before you with roads paved in gold. Your God asks that you make sacrifices in his name." He slowly pulled me further and further away from my faith. He pocked holes into what I had learned from my Bible as a child. My beliefs slipped from my hands. I carried his seed for nine months and when our son was born we named him Isaac . . .

He said "just as my former God had asked Abraham to offer his son Isaac as sacrifice, we too would be called to do the same." He was an occultist fanatic. I followed his words but I ignored his calls for sacrifice. I started to believe that I had let him lead me astray but at that point my mind was so cluttered, I was unsure of what was true about religion from what wasn't true. Which side was right and by choosing to be with him and following him, had I chosen the wrong side.

When Isaac was a month old they disappeared. He had taken Isaac. I called the police they couldn't help me yet. I called all of his associates none had heard from them. I returned to my faith, I ran to my old church and prayed for hours. I dragged myself home weak from crying, as I opened my door the phone rang. It was his best friends' girlfriend, she was whispering; she knew where he had taken my baby, she said my baby was hurt and I should hurry. I called the police, they were finally able to help they sent over a squad car. When we arrived at the park near Carpenter Ave. there they were. My baby was on the ground beneath his feet, he stood above Isaac with a knife in his hand screaming "it didn't work". He cut my baby's throat. Isaac was dead. After all that I went on a rampage. That was the week I began killing men. I compiled a list of every man with the name Steven in the Bronx yellow pages. It was like I was able to kill Steven over and over again. I had killed 16 men before I was arrested . . . I'm off my meds tonight and I'm writing this letter so that people will understand the reasoning behind my actions, so they know that I wasn't crazy, so they know that I was scorned.

Signed,
Rosemary

My Dearest Obina . . .

That was how all of letters to him began. We were dating for two years when he popped the question. I was elated. Aside from being young, educated, and drop dead gorgeous; he was a prince. I mean literally he was a prince an Nigerian prince, not a "Coming to America" prince. He came from a family of affluence, he carried the title of prince. He father the Eze is involved with international trade and his mother has masters in Biology. I once asked him why doesn't his mother get her doctorate, his reply was. "Why be a doctor or a teacher when you can be a queen? As queen her duties are simple; she should be able to engage in stimulating conversation, to be beautiful and enjoy the fruits of my fathers' labor. He found that last part funny as did I. Based on our conversations about the family and it's dynamics I could tell that of the Queens five children he was her favorite. They had a special affection for one another, that's why it didn't surprise me when she got sick, he wanted to be by her side. He was gone for a month and a half when his letters stopped. I would write and write and write with no answer. I began to worry, after all it was Nigeria maybe he had been kidnapped or God forbid he was dead. Then my last letter came back *RETURN TO SENDER* in bright red capital letters. I was going to find out what was going on with my fiancé. I booked the first flight I could get to Legos. When I arrived I checked into the hotel showered, got sexy in an elegant way of course and paid a taxi man to be my driver for the day. When I arrived at the family home the gate man announced me. The entire family came outside to greet me and there he was "my man" safe and sound. He came from a beautiful family his mother was young and beautiful, his brothers well they were even more handsome than he was and there was a gorgeous

43

girl who I could only assume was a cousin or a girlfriend of one of his brothers'. Obina rushed toward me, he grabbed my arm and asked "what are you doing here?" I said I wanted to make sure you were alright since I hadn't heard from you and then I turned to his mother and said Your majesty, I see you're doing much better". She looked at me in confusion "My son who is this?" Can you believe that bastard said I was a school mate from the university. His fucking friend. He introduced me to his mother as his friend!? The girl I thought was his cousin he introduced her to me as his wife. I was so stunned I could barely speak. In the taxi ride to the hotel and during the plane ride home I was stuck in a catatonic state, bumbling the words "his wife" repeatedly. For a long time I was stuck in a depression. He destroyed my hope in black men.

Signed,
Back from Africa

Dear Dr. Dillard,

In no way do I consider myself really religious. I am a casual Christian, I only go to church on holidays and special occasion like wedding and christening. In fact I have a few issues with some of what's in the bible but when it comes to rearing children I walk hand in hand with the bible. "Spare the rod, spoil the child". I wish my ex had agreed with me on that. I was the disciplinarian, he wanted to be our son's friend. I always had to play the villain and he got to swoop in and play the hero. I wasn't trying to ruin our son's life, I was doing what a mother is suppose to do, protect her child. But thanks to his pampering, bending to our sons every will, our baby is gone.

I would say Anthony no you can't go out to night you have school in the morning you should be studying and my ex would say he's young let him go out, go out son and have fun; so his grades were low. If he disrespected a teacher I would say Anthony you have to respect authority, you will apologize and no fun for the next two weeks; my ex would say he's young he'll grow out of it and when I'd leave for work he'd let Anthony run the streets. Anthony started selling weed I wanted to send him to boarding school, my ex insisted he was going through a faze. When Anthony was murdered on those streets I didn't cry because I knew he was a brat and for the first time my ex had nothing to say. Spare the rod, spoil the child. It's hard enough influencing you children to do the right thing it's even harder when you have some one who has power over your child that upholds what he or she does wrong. The night after the funeral my ex came over and cried himself to sleep. While he slept I cut his throat as I asked "Is this a phase? Will I grow out of my need to grieve for my child? Will I grow out of it like our son should have grow out of the things he did?" I punished him for my child's death. I now reside in a cell, this is my punishment for not be a strong mother.

Signed,
The Rod

Part 4

The Finale

For the women reading this, sometimes you get a genuinely good man and you take him for granted. You take his loving nature for weakness, stop it! Allow him to love you because once he's gone you won't get him back and by cheating and mistreating him or whatever you did to make him leave you maybe destroying a potentially great man. Lets give credit to where credit is due; men become what women refer to as "dogs" when they have had a bad experience with a woman.

For the men reading this: though some women my come close, a woman who is truly and completely dedicated to you only comes once in a lifetime. If you are lucky enough to find that perfect woman, cherish her.

An Ode to My Shawty,

To my beautiful chocolate rose
It was you who defined these words I now speak
You gave me a joy that made other chicks envy
You were my charm
You were my peace
My pride . . .

For me you were the one
Perfection
To me there was only you, 'cause you were right
You made me a selfish man.
After all why should I have to share you
My chocolate rose

My chocolate rose
You taught me that love is art
To love . . .
I was no longer reluctant

I made you my heart, without which I could not live
I made you my soul and became closer to God
But you became my hate
Turning me into a bitter man

Your body was my temple
It began to crumble when you allowed the unworthy
to enter
You . . .
You laid waste to my fertile land, a place where my seeds
were to be sowed
Now that land is over run by weeds, slander, whispers
and rumors
A shame you created, now wallow in your creation.

My chocolate rose . . .

Dr. Dillard I was in love with this chick. She was the first chick I ever loved. The poem started out as a Valentines Day gift because I wanted to do something sweet for her and I tried my hand at poetry 'cause I know females like that type of thing. I found out this chick, this girl I considered my wife was sleeping with my brothers, my cousin and a few of my friends, even a couple of my enemies. I was hurt. I feel like I'm dying, my soul ran away so I'm going to hell that's if I'm not there already. Visions of me strangling her play in my head over and over again. It got so bad that one day I went to her crib and waited for her to come home and when she got there I flew into a rage and began choking her, then a broke free of my anger when I realized I almost killed her. I walked away breathless. Peace Dr. Dillard.

Signed,
Young Poet

Dear Dr. Dillard,

In this day and age, it's amazing to me how powerful racism still is. This is America our country is suppose to represent freedom and equality amongst all people but in some instances we find ourselves being judged by the amount of pigment in our skin. To my loved ones I am a beautiful representation of what two races can become by unifying themselves. To those who remain blinded by ignorance and hatred, I am considered as an abomination.

I was in love with a down home country boy, he loved me in the way I had always hoped to be loved. He was from Alabama, I should have known better but I was raised not to see ones color but their character. He asked me to marry him and when I accepted he wanted to take me home to meet his mother.

We were suppose to spend the weekend but our stay together ended on the day we arrived. His home was small and modest, his mother greeted us in the front yard. She welcomed me with open arms. She escorted me to the porch, offered me a seat and something to drink; then she asked "Billy" to join her in the house. I could over hear their conversation. She said "Billy what were you thinking? Bringing her here. You know how your father feels about these things, mixing the races". Then "Billy" said "I think once daddy meets her, he'll see how beautiful and intelligent she is and then he'll have no choice but to love her." Billy came back outside. I acted as if I hadn't heard what had just been said.. He smiled at me uneasily and kissed my forehead.

We sat and talked for hours, just the three of us. I helped his mom in the kitchen. I took a liking to her, she was very forthcoming with me. She said "Darling, I like you and I would be honored to be your mother in-law because you make my son happy but I have to tell you, so that you're not caught off guard. Billy's daddy hates anyone that's not white. If I knew who he really was before I fell in love with him, we wouldn't be standing here talking to you. So what ever you hear today don't let it get you down and don't you cry. I'm not strong enough to stand up to him. I was astonished by what she said. All I could do was shake my head.

As we sat down to eat dinner, Bill's father walked in, the room became quiet and then erupted with the sound of his voice." What in the hell is going on here? And who in the hell is this?"Billy stood up and said daddy this is my fiancé M . . .

Fiancé!? Did I hear you right, boy? I know you aint talking about this thing sitting at my dinner table. I stood up to defend myself. Who are you calling a thing?

49

He said "I'm talking to you! The only half nigger, chink cunt bag bitch in the room. Get the hell out of my house before I'm forced to use my riffle. Billy started to follow me as I walked out, his father stopped him. Boy if you leave with that mongrel bitch you'll be disowned, you'll never step another foot in this house again. Billy's pace slowed as he looked at me then he looked at his mother and then he stopped completely. He looked at me with tears in his eyes and said I'm sorry baby but my mother needs me and if I leave she stuck here with him. That was the last time I saw him.

Signed,
The Wrong Color

Dear Dr. Dillard,

I have to write because I can't speak, not by choice and NO! I wasn't born mute. My tongue was cut from my month by the sick freaks that lived upstairs from me. They kidnapped me and held me hostage for a month. I was missing for an entire month and you mean to tell me there were no leads, no anonymous calls, nothing. See I know that racism exists but who would have known that the government that is put here to protect you and I aren't here to protect you or I. They really don't care about us. When little white girls are kidnapped or run away you see their faces plastered all over the news, on every radio station, flyers are posted every where, the police canvas the streets for weeks. But not for us, when Blacks and Latinos go missing we get dismissed. I was gone a month, you know what I got? A two minute spot on the Bronx News. Screw the government. That's not why I'm writing though. I want you to know why I fear and hate white people and blacks (my own kind). The interracial couple upstairs snatched me as I tried to enter my apartment. The situation was so surreal. They were a couple of freaks. During the day while her husband was at work she'd stick me with cigarettes, cut my arms and legs with a dirty razor and sometimes she'd come into the room naked(they kept me in a windowless half bedroom), she'd tie me to the bed and sit on my face. While I was gasping for air she'd grew more aroused by the possibility of me suffocating underneath her old soured vagina. It was during one of those times that I screamed and called out for help. As punishment she cut off my tongue and as an extra bonus she took my pinkies too. Her husband had enough crazy for the both of them. When he saw what she did, he beat her up in front of me. He started to talk to me like I was his baby, rubbing my head, dressing my injuries. Then he broke my jaw and asked if it hurt less than what his wife did to me? He sodomized me, he broke two of my ribs and locked me in a large dog cage. "When you act like a good little girl you can sleep in your bed." he said. After that he and Mrs. Crazy Coo would have sex in front of the cage and make me watch he'd dig his nails into her back until you could see blood she'd bight her lip and scream harder! They were really sick. I fell ill. My body was rotting in my own fesses and the infection from my wounds. I didn't think I would get out of that apartment. I did though or else I wouldn't be writing to you today. I passed out, my pulse was so faint that they could detect it and I guess they assumed I was dead. They left me in front of my apartment door for my mother to find. She found me on the brink of death. I was in comma for a week. When I woke up I wrote out my account of what happened for the police. The couple wasn't arrested though, they packed there things and left when they realized the ambulance in the front of the building was for me. I don't leave the house because I fear they might come for me again. I would love to be able to take from them what they took from me. Not my tongue. Not my thumbs. But my freedom.

Signed, Captive

Dear Dr. Dillard,

You're women. Would you please tell me. Why woman feel only they can be victims? Men do this, men do that, all men are dogs. But you never hear about the crap they do. Woman cheat, woman deceive as a matter of fact woman are a lot better at it than we are. Real talk, woman make men what they are. No man is born bad, that's just how they're molded over time. Take me for example. I loved this girl whole heartedly, she had me open. It was that serious that when I went a week without seeing her I felt physical pain. That's word to everything I love. She was the one I wanted to marry and have children with. And I did, I married her because it was what I wanted to do. I didn't want to father illegitimate children with the woman I loved. She got pregnant a few months after we got married. I put all my hopes and dreams into her belly. That baby straightened out my life. I stopped hustling. I went back to school. I got a 9 to 5, I became a square. When my little girl was born she was the most perfect baby I had ever seen. She had her mother's eyes, her mouth she had it all. She was a more beautiful version of her mother. That little girl was my only reason for getting up in the morning.

When my little girl got sick, my world ended. She needed marrow. I was the first to volunteer. It was my duty to protect her and that was what I was trying to do. To add insult to injury, our blood didn't match. If she's mine that didn't make sense. I demanded they retest us, they had to have mixed up our blood with some one else's. When it came back the same, I requested a DNA test. A piece of paper had to tell me my little girl wasn't my little girl. I didn't cry, I broke down and sobbed. That wasn't the tip of the iceberg; she was my cousins' baby, my cousin!

Signed,
Daddy

Dear Dr. Dillard,

Tradition! Tradition! Tradition! That's all I use to hear from my parents. Marry a Dominican man. Casate con tu raza (marry your own). They'd say. It was always in Spanish. I told them I'm American, this is America, speak to me in English. No hablo espanol ! I'd fire back. When you gonna give us grandchildren, I was eighteen at the time, I was looking to go to college and they wanted me to get married and reproduce like a rabbit. My mother would go on and on about how by my age she was married and pregnant with my brother Manny. That's not what I wanted for myself.

My father's best friend's son had just come from D.R. and he was looking for a wife, our parents pushed us together. I finally gave in and married Haciel. I wasn't sure how we were going to work because he was always speaking Spanish and I don't. I understand it but I don't speak it. I kept telling him that and like my parents he'd tell me I should be ashamed of myself, a Dominican girl that can't speak Spanish. He was always telling me to cook, I can't cook either. I'd tell him, that he knew all those things before he married me so he has no choice but to deal with it. When I turned twenty—one I had a set of twin girls, from there the arguments got worse. He loved them but he had a problem with them being girls. Where are my sons, you don't do anything else, you should at least be able to give me a son. I ask you for boys you give me girls you can't do anything right. He always said this. I told him I wanted to back to school. Once again in Spanish he said "?Tienes trabajo para pagan estudios? (Do you have a job to pay for this school?) I work and you stay home with your babies, that's how it works in my house". He started to beat me up, I'd fight back but I'm small and couldn't do much damage. We would have make up sex after the fights and he'd make me do dirty things like make me put my finger in his ass to make him cum. I told my mother what was going on and she told me there was nothing I could do that was what marriage was. I was so unhappy. Doctor is everything I tell between me and you? Because you're like a real doctor and in a way I'm your patient right? So whatever I tell now is just between us, right?

One night he wanted to do some freak shit, like bondage. He pulled a belt around his neck but it was to tight and he started to chock. I knew that if I helped him he'd own my life forever. I let him choke, I watched his soul leave his body. I watched my husband choke to death and I didn't feel any remorse. I waited about an hour before calling the police. When they got to our apartment I told them I had come in and found him like that. His finger prints were the only ones on the belt so the case was closed without question.

Signed,
La Princessa

Dear Dr. Dillard,

M-I-S-T-R-E-S-S, definition: a woman with whom a man has a usually long-term extramarital sexual relationship, often one in which he provides financial support.

That's what I was. His mistress or his kept woman. For thirteen years that was my duty. My man was married to another woman for fifteen years and had three children with her. I was the one on the side and had three children with him as well. He provided for us all. She lived in a house with him and their children and I lived in a three bedroom apartment with our children. I had to settle for seeing him for a few hours in the evening, we very rarely saw him on the weekends because the weekends and holidays were for his legitimate family. I had to put up with the situation because it was the only thing that could be expected. She didn't find out about our family/ his other family until the situation became to much for my eldest daughter, she was tired of being what she called a second class citizen. She called his wife and told her everything. She thought by doing so he'd would end up leaving her and their children and move in with us so we could finally be a family. Her plan ended up backfiring but the outcome was a lot worse than what I thought it would be. He chose his wife and their kids over us. He stopped coming by, he changed his numbers, he stopped paying our rent and the children's private school fees. He cut us off completely. He called before moving his family out of state. He said "for thirteen years we had a good thing going but I let my daughter (our daughter mind you) mess it up and the most important thing to him is wife and their children's happiness. If he had to sacrifice the happiness of me and my children in order to do so that's what he was going to do." He surely did.

We are struggling my kids have to go to public school for the first time in their lives, I had to find a job and we no longer see him or hear from him. That's the life of a mistress. Today I'm finally getting even. The courts found him and I have been awarded back child support this included the years we wee still together.

Signed,
The Kept Woman

Dear Dr. Dillard,

Tell me how you protect the one you love from another person you love? Why do you have to chose between the two? I'm a mother I raised my son for eight years with no help from his father. And for eight years I stayed single because the minute most men hear you have a child they head straight for the hills. So naturally when I found a man that was willing to overlook the fact that I had a kid, I held on for dear life. I wasn't going to let him go for anything or anyone.

I can't lie there were signs that something strange was going on in my home but who could pin point what it was exactly. Well maybe I did know what was going on. But for me to acknowledge it would mean I'd be alone again and I didn't want to be alone anymore.

What you've just read was what my mother told her psychiatrist. On my seventeenth birthday I got drunk and broke into her psychiatrist's office to steal her file. That was what she told him. I can't believe her, that bitch! She tried to sugar coat what really happened, the only part that was really true was when she said she wasn't going to let her man go for anyone. That was very true. You wanna hear something that would mess up any kids head? My mom caught her "man" molesting me a few times and she didn't do anything about it. I know night after night she heard me crying in my room while her "man" was mounting me. I'd wake up in the mornings with blood in my boxers, boys should never have blood in their underwear, I felt like a girl seeing her period. A girl seeing her period is a reminder to her that she's a woman, the blood I saw every morning reminded me that I was some ones bitch, a fish for a shark. Can you call her a mother? She blamed me for not having a love life but I never asked to be born, I wasn't the one who told her to sleep with my dead beat father and get knocked up. That was all her, she made those choices. The day I told her I didn't want him to hurt me anymore, I gave her a choice. It was either he goes or I go. She chose him. She handed me over to my grandmother. She wouldn't even call me to check up on me. Great mom, huh? I think I'm the first kid in history to say I hate my mother and mean it. As I grew older my hatred for grew. I couldn't maintain normal relationships. I'm so heavily medicated I cant keep a job. But I'm through feeling sorry for myself, I'm through with cursing her name, I was through with seeing my step fathers face in my nightmares. I am now screaming as I write this letter to you Dr. Dillard. I'm mailing this letter to you before I go over to her house tonight. It brings me some comfort to share my plans with you because this is the night I will free myself from my meaningless life. When I get to the house I will gauge out her eyes, cut her breast from her body, then I will silence her with the same pillow her husband used to muffle my cries at night and when her body stops jerking, I will sit waiting for husband to come home. When he arrives I with cut off his dick and place it into is mouth so that he will understand how little pleasure he had to offer.

Signed,
Fish

Dear Reader,

Okay you've made it to the end. At this point it's alright to tell you the truth about the conception of this book. I also know that you've figured out that Dr. Sarah Dillard is a fictional representation of myself.

First, the idea for this book came to me after a horrible breakup. He was a womanizer; the break up was what I like to refer to as a hood drama. Childish games of phone tag with other women and direct confrontations. It was very dramatic and a grave waste of precious time. I'm best known for finalizing a break up with a break up letter. This letter allows you to vent, it allows you to say all that you should have said, before you told him it was over. It's like kicking him when he's down, just to let him know he screwed up and lost a good thing. That letter was filled with verbal explosives. Excuse me as I have taken a moment to laugh. As I was saying, once I reached the end of my nasty letter, it dawned on me that there was no point in the letter. I'm older, this isn't grade school, and I've grown. The letter was unnecessary because life could have dealt me a worse set of cards. From there my mind was overrun with crazy possibilities and outrageous scenarios. I had started to think about other relationships, things I had been told, witnessed or heard about relationships. Things that my friends or family members had gone through were big contributors to my thought process.

For those of you who are wondering "Is any of this real?" The answer to that is . . . Only a select few of the accounts represent actual events (with some added embellishments, of course). From those events Keith's wife, So gone and later Kerry were born. I stopped writing and about three years later while going through some old computer files I came across Keith's wife and decided to finish the accounts.

This book is my first, it is my baby. It was meant to be short so as not to bore you and I believe it is the perfect length for non—readers (people that hate to read books of any kind). You know what forget about what I just said; this book was meant for everyone. I hope you enjoyed the book, I also hope that it has opened your eyes. I like keeping things brief and interesting. That being said I won't take up anymore of your time. Peace. One.

Signed,
Jeh Wells

About the Author

I have never been good at discussing myself. In fact I blush when paid a compliment. What can I say? I am a plain Jane. I adore my family and friends. My favorite author is Henry W. Longfellow. On the weekends I like to eat pasta while listening to 30 Seconds to Mars. As I write this I am smiling softly to myself because the way the sun is kisses my neck tells me spring is coming.